Lucy and the Leprechaun's Rainbow

Lucy and the Leprechaun's Rainbow

Sharon Gardner Fischer

VANTAGE PRESS
New York

Illustrated by Kate Gartner

FIRST EDITION

Published by Vantage Press, Inc.
516 West 34th Street, New York, New York 10001

Manufactured in the United States of America
ISBN: 0-533-09513-1

0 9 8 7 6 5 4 3 2 1

To the young cancer patients, especially at N.I.H., my hope and heroes, and to the members of Candlelighters, all of whom in learning to rely upon as well to give to others have truly embraced friendship on the most significant of levels.

A special thanks to Bud, JoAnne, Rob, Steve and Holly, my fax and true friend, all of whom were indispensable in the workings of this book, as well as to Marty, my mentor, and Ekki, my golden guy.

Lucy and the Leprechaun's Rainbow

Chapter 1

Lucy couldn't wait to go to bed! She had lost her last tooth, and that of course meant that the Tooth Fairy would leave her some money. And Lucy liked money! She'd been saving coins in her piggy bank all year, and now that Christmas was only two weeks away, she thought she might just have enough for that beautiful doll she'd seen in the store window.

"In case Santa forgets to bring it," she told herself.

Of course, she also planned to buy presents for her parents.

Lucy carefully placed the tooth under her pillow and then made a wish out loud in the dark: "I wish the Tooth Fairy would bring me two quarters or a half-dollar. Whichever is easier for her to carry."

"A half-dollar? Ha!" said a high, squeaky voice.

Lucy quickly sat up in bed.

"Who said that? Who's there?!" she asked, squinting in the darkness.

"I can show you a lot more money than *that*, my dear!" the voice cried.

"Where are you? Are you the Tooth Fairy? I can't see you!" Lucy said.

"Then turn the lights on!" the voice answered.

"But then my parents will come in."

"Oh, what a bother! Now, let me think!" The voice cackled. "Ah, yes! Here we are:

"Crackle! Crinkle! Sprackle! Sprinkle!
Like the stars I now will twinkle!
By the rays of Rainbow's light,
You shall see me in the night!"

And suddenly, Lucy could see tiny particles of light, blowing up into the air like dust. Slowly, they gathered into a shape, and finally, there stood a little man, no bigger than one of Lucy's dolls! He was dressed in a little green jacket and knee-high pants, with black stockings and boots that curled up at the toes. On his head was a gleaming black hat, which bent and dangled over his left shoulder.

"You don't look like the Tooth Fairy. Are you an elf?" Lucy asked.

"A tooth fairy! An elf! Ha!" the little man snickered. "I'm a leprechaun, child! Don't you recognize one when you see one?!"

"I—don't know," Lucy stammered. "I guess I've never seen one."

"Well, now you have. Hubert's my name, gold's my game!" he said, putting his tiny hands on his hips.

"What do you mean?" Lucy asked.

"By the Blarney Stone! Humans, and a child of all things!" Hubert threw up his hands. He scratched his chin and tiptoed over to Lucy's bed. "What I mean, my dear," he whispered, "is that I know where there is plenty of gold! All I need is for you to do me a teensy-weensy little favor! How would you like a real gold piece instead of a silly half-dollar?"

"Oh! I've never even seen a real gold piece!" Lucy said.

"My, my, this is your night," said Hubert, snickering. "First a leprechaun, then a gold piece. Okay then, listen closely."

Wide-eyed, Lucy leaned forward toward the leprechaun.

"Tonight, very soon, there's going to be a rainbow, right here in your room!" Hubert said.

"Here? At night? Wow! Wait'll I tell everybody in school tomorrow! They won't believe it!" Lucy cried.

"That's right!" Hubert said sternly. "Nor will they believe anything else that you're going to see tonight. That's why you must vow, by the Blarney Stone, not to tell anyone a thing about our little agreement. Do you vow it?"

"By the Blarney Stone, whatever that means!" Lucy said.

"Okay then," Hubert continued. "You have only to climb the steps to the crest of the rainbow—"

"Steps?! Who's ever heard of steps on a rainbow?" Lucy said.

"This is a special rainbow. It will do anything I tell it to do, and steps will appear when I wish," Hubert hastily explained. "Now then," he continued, "when you've reached the top of the rainbow, slide down, and at the very bottom is my pot of gold. It even has my name on it, as I recall."

"Wow! Your own pot of gold!" Lucy said.

"Stop interrupting!" Hubert scolded. "Now then, when you've reached the bottom, stuff as much of the gold as you can into your bathrobe pockets—more than that you will not be able to carry. Steps will appear on the other side as you turn to come back again. When you've arrived home, place the gold pieces on the windowsill to dry, and in the morning there will be one left, for you to keep."

"Only one?" Lucy asked.

"Don't push your luck!" Hubert said. "Each piece is worth more than all those silly coins in your piggy bank! Now are you willing?" he asked. "Do you understand what you are to do?"

"Oh, yes!" Lucy replied.

"Okay then, I must be off now! Happy landing, my dear!" With that, the window flew open, and as Hubert disappeared into the night, Lucy thought she heard someone singing a funny little song:

"Away I hop! Along I skip!
I'll have my gold, I'll sail my ship!
These silly folks, who are such fools,
Don't know I play by Hubert's rules!"

Chapter 2

Lucy got up and put on her bathrobe. But suddenly, she had an idea!

"What if I took a big bucket along? What if I bring back even more gold than Hubert asked for? Then I bet he'd give me more than just one gold piece to keep!"

She quickly reached into her closet and fumbled around for the big basket of toys and seashore playthings. Finally, she pulled out a large, plastic sand bucket.

When she turned around, the rainbow was already there, pushing through her window. With the bucket over one arm, she climbed out and started up the rainbow's steps. Colors shimmered in the dark beneath her feet, and she felt as light as a feather as she walked along. She wanted to see how high up she was and tried to peer over the rainbow's edge, but it was far too wide. To her left, she could see only as far as the color yellow, and to her right, the color blue.

Suddenly the steps ended, and Lucy knew she had reached the top. She sat, and began to slide down the rainbow's shaft. She flew! Cool air whistled in her ears and tickled her hands and feet. It was fantastic! So slippery-smooth! *This is like the biggest water slide I've ever seen! Or a giant roller coaster! Or even better!* she thought.

A wave of colors shone and flashed before her. To her left, red, orange, and yellow warmed the sky, and to her right, blue-green and violets glimmered beneath twinkling stars. Just when Lucy was beginning to think the rainbow might never end: Kerplunk! Plink! Plunk! She landed right in the middle of a huge pot, with gleaming, golden nuggets jingling all around her.

"Whew!" Lucy said, as she boosted herself up by the rim of the pot. The gold pieces scraped against each other and slipped beneath her feet, but she was finally able to stand. Then, still holding onto the rim, she carefully leaned over and read: *pโoโ s๚əqnH* or *Hubert's gold*, when read right-side up.

Lucy looked up at the sky, already beginning to grow light, and hurriedly filled her pockets and the bucket with gold.

I wish I had time to stay and have a look around! she thought.

"Lucy, please don't go yet!" said a voice from above.

Lucy looked up and saw a giant glowing green bird circling over her.

"Who are you?" Lucy asked.

"I am Fliega," called the beautiful creature. "I

belong to the family of the Rainfalcons. May I land?"

"Oh, yes!" Lucy cried. The bird swooped its way down in circles toward Lucy and perched on the rainbow's nearest step.

"But how did you know my name?" Lucy asked.

"We Rainfalcons fly far and as fast as the wind. We see and know many things," Fliega replied. "And now, Lucy, you will excuse me while I dry out my feathers." With that, Fliega stretched out her long, sparkling wings, which were drenched with rainwater.

"Fliega, you're soaking wet! But it's not even raining!" Lucy said.

"That's what you think! It's raining throughout most of this land, and it has been for a long time. It'll start here, too, and soon." They looked up at the sky, where dark clouds were already beginning to gather.

"You have come for Hubert's gold, have you not?"

Lucy nodded.

"Then let me advise you, if I may," Fliega said. "Hubert and his gold are no longer safe here. Please warn him, if you see him again. He will understand why."

"Hubert's in trouble?" Lucy asked.

"Hubert's always in trouble," said Fliega, chuckling. "And I must say, much of it he brings upon himself. He means well, but he loves to play tricks, and he's not always honest. You'd do well to

11

hide your gold piece from him, or you may be left with nothing."

"He would steal? From me? But I'm doing him a favor," Lucy said.

"Such is the way of leprechauns, and especially Hubert. Our last king placed the rainbow in Hubert's care hoping it would teach him responsibility, but he's never been able to give up his tricks." Fliega glanced upward.

"We haven't much time," she said. "I can say only this: We are all in danger here, and our land will soon no longer be safe anywhere. The king's throne has fallen into evil hands, and the new rulers are especially angry with Hubert and his rainbow."

"What's Hubert done?" Lucy asked.

"I haven't time to explain, but we need his help." Fliega said. "I couldn't expect you to return and help those who are here, though we would be thankful for your help, too. But I would appreciate your delivering my message to Hubert, should you see him again. I think the reason he asked you to help him out is that he's really looking for a friend. He just doesn't know how to go about it." Fliega sighed.

"If only Hubert understood that there are those here who care about *him*, and not his riches. Perhaps you might remind him of this, Lucy: real treasure is to be discovered in friendship, not in gold or a piggy bank."

Suddenly there came a cawing sound and,

12

looking up, Lucy saw nearly a dozen other giant birds, all in vibrant colors of the rainbow. Thunder clapped, and a streak of lighting crossed overhead. "I must go now, and you, too, Lucy! Careful crossing that rainbow!" And with a flutter of wings, Fliega was gone.

Lucy pushed herself up out of the pot of gold and started up the rainbow's stairs, but the climb was not nearly so easy this time. The gold seemed to grow heavier with every step, and her bathrobe pockets stretched and dragged against the surface as she trudged along. It began to rain, and strong winds blew up over the rainbow's crest, pushing Lucy farther and farther toward the edge. The bucket over her arm suddenly began swinging wildly in the wind, and tipped, spilling the gold as easily as though it were water. But Lucy was too worried to even notice.

After what seemed like hours, she finally stumbled upon the last step. A gust of wind whipped around her, making a last attempt to knock her over. Lucy fell, and slid on her stomach, face-first down the other side of the rainbow. The cold wind slapped her face and stung her eyes as she went, until at last, she shot through her window and landed in bed.

Chapter 3

Lucy awoke the next morning in a panic. She had been so tired the night before that she'd forgotten to hide her gold piece.

She sprang out of bed and peered into the bucket, which was now filled with nothing but water.

"Hubert tricked me!" she cried.

"Ah, but you tried to trick me first!"

Lucy whirled around to find Hubert standing next to her closet.

"I only wanted to bring back some extra gold," she said.

"But I told you you couldn't carry more than two pockets full. And now my gold is spilled! I'll never find it all! Never!"

"I'm sorry, Hubert," Lucy apologized. Then she remembered Fliega, and she quickly delivered the Rainfalcon's message.

"I already knew it, I did!" Hubert stamped his tiny boot on the floor. But then a great sorrow appeared on his face. "Is it swampland yet?" he asked mournfully.

"What do you mean? I didn't see too much," Lucy said.

"There are mighty mean folk who are trying to turn our land into swamp, and , and . . . " Hubert looked as though he were about to cry.

"What's the matter, Hubert? Tell me. Fliega couldn't."

"Oh, I've played a trick! A terrible trick! And now they'll all be punished for it, and I'm to blame!" he cried.

"Hubert! What did you do?" Lucy cried. "Tell me!"

"My rainbow can't live without the sun, Lucy. And all those who live there—Willy and Fia and Gumper, and even the Rainfalcons and all the others—they can't survive in swampland, with nothing but rain."

"Then you've got to help them!" Lucy said.

"By the Blarney Stone, child! The water would be over me head by now!"

"But they're your friends!" Lucy said.

"I've got to save me rainbow! We all need it, we do! I've got to hide it! By the Blarney Stone! I've got to hide meself! They'll be looking for me!"

"I'll help you!" Lucy cried. "Fliega said they could use my help! You can stay here with me, Hubert! Come to school with me! I don't know how to hide your rainbow, but you can fit right into my coat pocket!"

Hubert looked so sad. He was too tired and troubled to even protest as Lucy slipped him into her coat pocket before leaving for school.

Chapter 4

When Lucy entered her classroom, she didn't hang her coat in the coat closet as the other children did, but draped it carefully over her chair, so that Hubert wouldn't be crushed or discovered.

Their teacher, Miss Sims, greeted the children, and then, looking at Lucy, said, "Lucy, you know where we hang our coats. Why is yours on your chair?"

"I—I have a cold, Miss Sims."

"Oh, dear. Well, you'd better wear your coat then, if you start to feel too cool."

Lucy stood up and put her coat on. From inside her pocket, she could hear Hubert sadly mumbling: "All me gold, and all me magic, and nothing I can do."

She quickly tugged at the pocket to get Hubert to settle down. Didn't leprechauns know how to be quiet?

Suddenly, Lucy noticed a new boy, standing next to Miss Sims.

"We have a new student, boys and girls. I'd like you all to say hello to Andrew," Miss Sims said.

Lucy couldn't help noticing something different about Andrew. He seemed so thin and pale,

compared to her other classmates. And at recess, Lucy heard Andrew tell Miss Sims that he would rather stay indoors, instead of going out to play with the others.

"All right, then," Miss Sims said. "You can keep Lucy company. We don't want her going outdoors with a cold."

Lucy was angry that she had to remain indoors during recess and wondered why Andrew would choose to do so.

"There's something wrong with that boy!" Hubert whispered from inside Lucy's pocket.

"Shhh!" Lucy told Hubert.

"But I didn't say anything," Andrew said, thinking that Lucy had been talking to him.

"Oh! I didn't mean *you!*" Lucy said, now angry at Hubert.

"All me gold, and all me magic . . . " Hubert started mumbling again.

"What did you say?" Andrew asked Lucy.

"I didn't say anything," Lucy said. "But, how come you don't want to play outside with the others? It's snowing, and I'll bet they're making snowballs and snow forts and everything. I wish I could go out!"

"I just don't feel like it," Andrew said quietly.

"He's lying! Lyyyyying!" Hubert hissed.

"I am not lying!" Andrew said. "I mean, I *want* to play outside, but I can't. My coat—it's kind of old and torn up on the inside—it just gets so cold, and . . . " Just then, Miss Sims and the other students filed into the room.

Lucy couldn't help thinking about Andrew throughout the day. How horrible not to be able to play outside in the snow!

At the end of the day, Miss Sims instructed the children each to write their name on a piece of paper, which she then collected and placed into a hat.

"Boys and girls," she said, "you all know that we're going to have a gift exchange at our Christmas party this Friday. I'd like for you each to draw one name from the hat, and that is the person for whom you'll buy a gift."

Suddenly Lucy had a wonderful idea! She remembered Fliega's words and thought about all the coins in her piggy bank. She tugged at her pocket. "Hubert! You've got to help me somehow!"

"How's that?" the leprechaun said.

"We're drawing names from the hat! You've got to use your magic somehow and help me to draw Andrew's name! I want to buy him a coat for Christmas!"

"Whatever for? A boy who lies—"

"Hubert! Please! He needs it, so he can play outside. And—and I'd like to be his friend."

"Friend," Hubert echoed sadly. "Oh, what a bother! Let me think now!"

Lucy heard him mutter something, snap his fingers, and then, "Lucy, your wish is Hubert's command."

"Thank you, Hubert!" Lucy cried. She raced over to the hat and was overjoyed when she read Andrew's name.

Chapter 5

When Lucy arrived home from school, her mother agreed to take her shopping that very afternoon. She raced up the stairs to her bedroom and broke open her piggy bank. The coins rolled all over the floor, and she and Hubert scurried to scoop them up and put them into her purse.

"You'd better stay here, Hubert. The stores will be crowded. We don't want anyone to bump into you," Lucy said. Hubert wasn't pleased, but he said nothing as Lucy placed him inside her closet and closed the door.

At the store, there were so many coats that Lucy didn't know which one to choose. She had already bought presents for her parents and grandparents, and Miss Sims, and her best friend, Jenny. Finally she selected a handsome brown jacket, with warm, wooly lining, and took it to the counter.

"What do you have there, Lucy?" Her mother asked.

"It's a coat, for Andrew. You know, the new boy I told you about."

"Oh, Lucy. That's too expensive. You don't have enough money for a coat. Why don't you buy him

this nice scarf? It will help him to stay warm," her mother said.

The scarf looked so small and plain next to the jacket, but Lucy knew her mother was right. Any of these coats would cost much more than all the coins she'd ever saved in her piggy bank. The last of her coins, plus a few her mother gave her, were enough. She sadly took the scarf and left the store with her mother.

When they were home, Lucy quickly went to her closet to let Hubert out. She found him with his arms crossed, tapping his tiny foot on the floor. He scowled at her.

"Don't leave me here in the dark again! I hate it, I do!" he said.

"Hubert, you've got to help me! I need that gold piece you promised me. My coins weren't enough to buy Andrew the coat!"

Hubert hung his head in shame.

"Oh, Lucy! I would help you! No tricks, even. But my gold is worthless in your land," he said sorrowfully.

"But—you said just one piece is worth more than all my money!" Lucy said.

"And so it is!" he snapped, in his old tone again. A fiery glow appeared in his eyes. "But it can't be used as money."

"But I don't understand," Lucy said.

"I know, child. And I'm sorry. You've been so good to old Hubert, too."

Lucy moped through the next few days of the

week. Hubert was no comfort. He became jumpier every morning as his fear grew that he and his rainbow would be discovered by the "evil folk," as he called them.

Friday morning, Lucy wrapped the scarf and went upstairs to get Hubert before leaving for school. She couldn't find him anywhere.

"Hubert! Hubert! Where are you? Don't play games! I've got to go to school!" she cried. Then suddenly, something on the windowsill caught her eye. A little golden chip glowed up at her, and golden dust, scattered on the windowsill, read:

> With winter's wind I now must leave,
> But I'll return on Full Moon's Eve.

And he didn't even say good-bye, Lucy thought sadly.

Chapter 6

The Christmas party was drawing to an end, and the children pranced about the room, happily delivering and opening their gifts. Only Lucy was unhappy. Hubert's disappearance, and the fact that she had only a scarf to give to Andrew, had left her in a gloomy mood.

Slowly, she walked over to Andrew's desk, and handed him the package.

"Thanks, Lucy!" Andrew smiled as he unwrapped the scarf. "I like it!"

Miss Sims spotted them, and walked over to them. "Andrew," she said, pointing, "it looks like there something more for you, there, in Lucy's package."

Andrew reached into the bag. A glimmer of light shone, as he started to pull something out. He continued to tug at the contents, and now everybody in the room turned to gaze at the package, radiating bright beams of light.

Finally, Andrew pulled out a glowing coat, fully lined and shimmering with all the colors of the rainbow! Andrew stood, staring at the beautiful coat, unable to speak. There was a silence in the classroom as the coat began to shine and glitter

like gold beneath the lights. Then suddenly, all the children raced to Andrew's side. They couldn't help admiring the gleaming colors and running their fingers over the silky threads.

"It's glowing! Look how it shines!" they cried. They all wanted to put the coat on, but Miss Sims insisted that Andrew try it on first, since it was his coat.

Shyly, Andrew slipped his arms into the armholes and buttoned the coat around him. "It fits perfectly! And it's so warm!" he exclaimed. His face seemed to light up as he smiled, for he no longer looked pale, with the coat's warmth glowing around him.

"It's fantastic! Look at all those colors!" the children cried.

"I have to say, I've never seen anything quite like it," Miss Sims said. "Wherever did you find such a coat, Lucy?"

Andrew had slipped the coat off and was squinting, trying to read the very teensy-weensy, tiny print on the label.

"What's it say? Read it out loud!" the others cried.

"It says," Andrew read:

> "A gift that's new,
> And yet so old,
> Of raindrop dew,
> And magic gold.
> Like friendship, its value
> Is sure to grow,
> Made by the company:
> H's Rainbow."